A Buck and A Puck

written by   J.L.W

Tellwell Talent
www.tellwell.ca

ISBN
978-0-2288-1584-6 (Hardcover)
978-0-2288-1585-3 (Paperback)

A Buck and a Puck

Nature Nurtures Storybooks

Lulu loves everything about hockey. She loves learning to skate. She loves learning to shoot the puck. She loves the smells and the sounds of the cold arena. But most of all, Lulu loves having fun with her friends. Saturday mornings in the winter are for hockey. Fun! Fun! Fun!

Aunt B and Mom are at the arena watching Lulu play today. Aunt B is Lulu's loving pup. She likes to sit on Mom's lap for the games.

Lulu is on the red team, so she has a red jersey. It has a big number four on the back. Lulu's best friend, Madolina Milenesi, is on the blue team. Her jersey number is nine. Madolina is very good at hockey. She scores a lot. Lulu has not scored yet this year, but she is trying.

Lulu is not happy. Madolina just took the puck from Lulu and scored her third goal of the game.

Today's final score is 6–0 for Madolina's blue team.

On the way home, Mom asks, "Why are you so upset, Lulu?"

"Maddy is a bad friend. She took the puck away from me," Lulu says.

Aunt B looks puzzled.

"That is how you play the game," Mom offers.

"But she already had two goals," Lulu sulks.

"If you want to play the game, you have to accept the way it is played. Do your best and be nice to Madolina for doing her best."

Suddenly, Lulu's mom stops the car. SCREEEECH!

Lulu sees a beautiful male deer with giant antlers. He is standing in the middle of the road, staring at them.

"WOW, a buck!" Lulu lets out in awe.

The big buck takes one leap and is off the road and gone, right over a fence.

"Did you see that, Lulu?" her mom asks. "Wasn't he gorgeous and strong and graceful?"

"He seemed so gentle," Lulu says, "and so big."

"Maybe we can learn something from the buck, Lulu," Mom says. "The buck is strong, yet he is gentle and kind." Her mom checks the road to make sure it is clear before driving again. "His kindness shows his strength. Showing kindness to people when we are angry or frustrated shows how strong we are on the inside. It is not always easy."

"Being kind makes me feel proud and strong, like the buck," Lulu adds.

"Very good, Lulu. I agree," Mom says. "Kindness can be powerful."

"I wonder if he can come to our next game?" Lulu giggles, her anger long gone. "A buck with a puck; a buck with a puck; a buck with a puck," she chants happily the rest of the way home.

The following Saturday arrives quickly. Dad calls up to Lulu from the kitchen, "Time to go, Lulu," and sings, "Where's your team spirit? Let me hear it!"

The blue team is winning again. Lulu knows that as long as she keeps trying, she will improve and hopefully score her first goal of the season.

Late in the game, Lulu is skating towards the puck excitedly. Suddenly—OOMPH—she is flat on her back looking up at the arena lights. Someone has just collided with her.

"GRRRR," says Lulu. She is angry.

Lulu rolls over to get up. She sees her best friend, Madolina, lying on the ice. Lulu remembers the beautiful strong buck. "Kindness shows strength," she reminds herself.

Lulu skates over to Maddy.

"Are you okay, Maddy?" Lulu asks, as she leans over her friend and offers to help her up.

Madolina sniffs back tears. "I'm sorry, Lulu. I fell."

Lulu pats Maddy on the back as they skate to the bench. The friends laugh. Lulu is feeling happy. She is glad she chose to be kind.

Lulu is so happy that on her next shift out on the ice, she shoots, and she scores!

The final score of today's game is 4–1 for the blue team. That is a big improvement for Lulu's red team.